The Power of Dragon Flame

The Junior Novelization

randomhouse.com/kids

ISBN 978-0-307-98231-5

Printed in the United States of America

10 9 8 7 6 5 4 3 2 1

nickelodeon™

The Power of Dragon Flame

The Junior Novelization

Adapted by J. E. Bright

Random House 🏠 New York

Chapter 1

"Bloom . . . ," a voice whispered worriedly. "Bloom . . . wake up."

A teenage girl with flaming red hair and bright blue eyes lay still on the floor of her living room. All around her were toppled furniture and smashed knickknacks. Behind her was a jagged, broken block of ice. The girl gingerly raised her head and saw through her teary eyes that her mother, Vanessa, and her father, Mike, were huddled around her, their faces creased with concern.

With a loud sob, she slumped forward into their arms and they held her comfortingly. "It's okay, Bloom. We're here," Bloom's mother murmured.

"Dad . . . Mom . . ." Bloom gasped. She couldn't finish her sentence. She was overwhelmed by everything she'd been through. She felt drained and horribly dizzy remembering the scene that had just taken place.

Bloom turned to look at her surroundings, and her eyes focused on the block of ice, which was completely out of place. There was an empty hole in the shape of Bloom's body in its center. Just moments before, the ice had encased Bloom, holding her captive, courtesy of a diabolical witch named Icy. Bloom wasn't sure how she had escaped, but somehow she had fallen out, onto the carpet.

Bloom shuddered as she remembered Icy and two other evil witches, Darcy and Stormy, attacking her in her parents' house in Gardenia. The three sister witches called themselves the Trix. They had been searching for a massive source of energy called the Dragon Flame—which they had found in Bloom. Bloom was actually a fairy, and had been attending Alfea College for Fairies on a planet called Magix until she had come home to Earth a day before.

The Trix had descended on Bloom's house, determined to capture her Dragon Flame using a magical vacuum that could suck the power out of a fairy. Bloom had just managed to keep her parents alive, and had barely survived herself.

Bloom hadn't been able to battle all three witches at once. While she was protecting her parents from Stormy and Darcy, Icy had sneaked up behind her and frozen her in ice. As Bloom struggled to free herself from her prison, the three Trix had cast a complicated spell on her.

"Vacuum!" they cried together.

In the most painful moment of her life, the spell had drained Bloom of her magical powers.

As they left, the Trix revealed to Bloom that she was the most powerful fairy in the Magic Dimension, with her power of the Dragon Flame . . . the power they had stolen from her. The horrible Trix had cackled gleefully at her misery as they teleported back to Cloudtower, the college for witches on Magix.

Her eyes brimming with tears, Bloom recalled why she had left Magix and Alfea College. She had

had it all. She had belonged to a group of fairy friends called the Winx Club that was absolutely fabulous. A prince named Sky, who attended Redfountain College in Magix, had liked her. But then she had been completely humiliated at a Redfountain exhibition, in front of all the magical people of Magix. Even worse, she'd gotten into a public fight with a fairy princess named Diaspro, who'd turned out to be *engaged* to Prince Sky.

Sky. Dashing, kind, sweet Sky. Brawny, blond, beautiful Prince Sky. Bloom had had a crush on him since the moment they met. Finding out that Sky had a fiancée had pushed Bloom over the edge. She'd ruined the exhibition and upset everyone. After that, Bloom couldn't think of a reason to stay at Alfea College and had gone home to her parents in non-magical Gardenia . . . without even saying goodbye to her fairy best friends.

Then the wicked Trix had followed Bloom to Gardenia, attacked her and her parents, and stolen her power.

"Bloom, we were so worried," Vanessa said, nuzzling her cheek against her daughter's.

Mike rubbed Bloom's back. "Darling," he said, "are you all right?"

"Yes, yes," Bloom said, reassuring them with a hug. As she held her parents tight, a wave of sadness came over her. Even though Vanessa and Mike were the best parents a girl could ask for, they were not her birth parents. Not long ago, Bloom found out that she had been adopted. Sixteen years earlier, a fireman named Mike had found her in a burning building. Mike was the only dad Bloom had ever known. Finding out that she was adopted had blown her mind wide open . . . as had learning that she had a powerful fairy sister named Daphne.

Bloom was fine with the fact that Mike and Vanessa weren't her birth parents. Mike had saved her from the fire, and he and his wife had raised Bloom as their own, with deep love and good guidance. Bloom would always love her family.

She hugged her parents more tightly . . . just as

a brilliant flash of light flared in the middle of the living room. "The Trix!" Bloom cried. "Oh, no, they're back!"

Vanessa let out a little cry of fear, clutching Bloom around her shoulders. Mike stepped in front of them, ready to protect his family.

A sunny fairy named Stella materialized in the light. She gasped in alarm when she saw Bloom, battered and tearstained, with the ice block behind her.

"Stella!" called Bloom. She was so happy to see her friend that she almost burst into tears again. Stella was the first fairy Bloom had met, and they had hit it off immediately. Their powers were naturally complementary, too, with Bloom's fiery Dragon Flame and Stella's bright power of the Shining Sun. Bloom was almost ashamed to tell Stella what had happened with the witches.

Stella hovered worriedly in front of Bloom. "Are you okay?"

"The Trix," Bloom whimpered. "They followed

me here. They attacked me! They were so strong . . . and they took my power!"

Vanessa sat back on her heels as Bloom stood up. "Bloom," said Vanessa in a frightened voice, "what do you want to do?"

Biting her lip, Bloom wrapped her arms around her body. Everything had become so complicated and difficult! She didn't know how to handle whatever came next. What was she supposed to do without her powers?

Stella fluttered closer to Bloom on her iridescent wings, smiling brightly with encouragement. "You can't let the Trix get away with this," she said. "You have to fight them, Bloom. Come back to Alfea with me." Her expression became more serious and determined. "If we all work together, I'm sure we'll find a way to get back at the Trix . . . and thwart their evil plans."

Bloom's mother and father stepped closer to her. She put an arm around each of them.

"We're with you, sweetie," Mike said, smiling.

Bloom rested her head momentarily on her father's shoulder. "Oh, I love you—" she began, but then she had to move her arms quickly as her pet rabbit, Kiko, hopped up for a hug, too. Kiko was still very upset about the battle with the Trix, and Bloom forgot her own troubles while she comforted the cute bunny.

After quickly packing up her belongings and saying a tearful goodbye to her parents, Bloom, with Stella's help, teleported back to Magix. They arrived outside the gates of Alfea College. High above, Alfea's beautiful purple and pink domes and spires sparkled in the sunlight, and the gates opened like a fan of blue flower petals as Bloom and Stella approached. They entered the school's familiar broad courtyard, and the gates fluttered closed behind them. Bloom had thought she was fine with leaving Alfea behind her forever, but now that she was back, it seemed to welcome her.

It felt like home.

Chapter 2

Stella brought Bloom back to their dorm suite, which they shared with the other Winx Club fairies—raven-haired Musa, Fairy of Music; gentle Flora, Fairy of Nature; and tech-savvy Tecna, Fairy of Technology. The other fairies were at classes. As she looked around, Bloom wondered what to do next.

"I think you should talk to Headmistress Faragonda," Stella suggested.

Talking to Miss Faragonda, the stern but caring leader of the fairy school, sounded like a terrific idea to Bloom, so she headed to the headmistress's office immediately.

The white-haired headmistress was eternally

busy, but she always had time for her students. Miss Faragonda welcomed Bloom into her warm, classically decorated office.

Her cranky assistant, Griselda, quickly fixed a pot of steaming tea.

"Here," Griselda growled, pouring tea into a delicate cup for Bloom. "Drink it while it's hot." She sniffed at Bloom's bedraggled and sorry state. "It'll do you good."

When they were settled into comfortable chairs, Headmistress Faragonda said, "All right, then. Would you like to tell me what happened, Bloom?"

Bloom bowed her head and wrung her hands in her lap. She began tentatively, "I'd decided to leave Alfea—"

"Oh, Bloom!" Miss Faragonda groaned.

"I was at home in Gardenia when the Trix attacked me!" Bloom continued, and Griselda inhaled sharply in alarm. "They used a powerful spell and . . . they took my powers! They took my Dragon Flame!"

After a pained second during which she absorbed that information, the headmistress leaned forward and crossed her arms on her ornate desk. "Bloom, this is very grave news. The Dragon Flame is one of the great powers of the Magic Dimension."

Bloom raised her head and gazed at Miss Faragonda, her eyes wide. "You knew I had the power of the Dragon Flame?"

"I suspected," admitted the headmistress, adjusting her eyeglasses. "And I thought you would have time to learn about yourself and your powers."

Sitting on the edge of her chair, Bloom pressed one hand to her chest. "But now Icy, Darcy, and Stormy control the power of the Dragon Flame!"

Miss Faragonda shook her head wearily. "This does not bode well for Magix," she said. Then she realized something frightening, and she stood up abruptly and walked over to the huge windows behind her desk. "Even the witches will not be safe," she said. "We must warn Griffin!"

Tipped off by Headmistress Faragonda, Miss Griffin—the head of the witches' college,

Cloudtower—rushed furiously through her school's dark, spooky castle. She was so angry that her feet didn't even touch the floor. She whooshed from her office in a tall tower to the students' dining room two towers over.

Most of the teenage witches were eating breakfast in high purple alcoves and dizzying green balconies around the tall atrium in the tower's core, visiting their friends to gossip and scheme.

Headmistress Griffin hurried to the top of the tower, near her usual dining table above all the student witches. From there she had an excellent view down the tower's open center and could protect her pupils from the power-mad Trix.

All the teenage witches gasped as the door to the tower burst open far below. Icy, Darcy, and Stormy strode in and posed in the center of the floor, looking smug.

Miss Griffin glared down at the troublemakers. "Oh, the insolence!" she sneered when she saw their pleased expressions.

The three Trix just smiled up at their headmistress, their arms crossed.

"So you've decided to grace us with your presence!" Miss Griffin said sarcastically. "Well—"

But before Miss Griffin could finish her sentence, Icy raised her arms and whirled a spiral of ice shards up the open tower. The frozen cyclone slammed into Miss Griffin, and she let out a cry of pain as she was knocked off her feet. She smashed into her dining table, breaking it to pieces, and collapsed on the floor of her balcony.

"Miss Griffin!" a green-haired senior witch cried, running with an older witch to the headmistress's side. "Are you all right?"

The older witch clenched her hands into fists and shouted at the Trix, "Your behavior is unacceptable!"

Down below, Stormy laughed, her lightning bolt–shaped tresses bouncing around her face. "And what are you going to do?" she taunted. "Give us detention?" Stormy's face became deadly serious, and her eyes glowed red. She grunted as she called upon her heightened weather powers. Dark purple rings of energy swirled around her, and when she waved her arms, an enormous dusty tornado gusted up the atrium.

The twisting cyclone was so violently strong that it blew all the teenage witches off their balconies, along with their tables and chairs and unfinished breakfasts. The students flailed in the circling wind, screaming in terror.

The two senior witches who had helped Miss Griffin were blasted upward, and they smashed through the tall stained-glass windows behind them, leaving the headmistress alone.

As the tornado died down, Miss Griffin leapt off her balcony and plummeted through the atrium amid her tumbling students. As she fell, she shot beams of green light at her screaming pupils, teleporting them to the ground. When they were all safe, she cast the same spell on herself, vanishing and reappearing on the floor behind the Trix.

Miss Griffin rose to her feet, placing her pointy high-heeled shoes firmly on the stone floor. Her eyes glowed electric green as she concentrated on creating a giant purple power sphere between her tensed hands. With nimble flair, she flung the sphere at the Trix.

Sensing the attack, Darcy whirled around and magically halted the power sphere before it hit her. With a twist of her hands, she shrank the sphere until it was only the size of a marble. Then she wriggled her fingers and the sphere vanished in a puff of smoke. Darcy smiled, quite pleased at the ease with which she had vanquished her headmistress's magic.

Icy took advantage of Miss Griffin's shock to attack her with a snowy whirlwind. The funnel of snow flung Miss Griffin backward, and she slammed into the tower wall. A crust of ice pinned her to the wall, holding her powerless and at the Trix's mercy.

With a smug smile, Icy said, "In case you haven't gotten it yet, Miss Griffin . . . *we're* in charge now!"

Meanwhile, in Bloom's cozy dorm room at Alfea, the Winx fairies had come back from classes to find Bloom sitting despondently on her bed. After a joyful reunion, her friends—Stella, Musa, Flora, and Tecna—and her faithful bunny, Kiko, sat on her bed with her and listened to her tell the whole story of why she had run away . . . and the disaster that had followed.

Her friends nodded sympathetically as Bloom described her fight with the Trix in her parents' house, and they gasped when Bloom explained how Icy, Stormy, and Darcy had drained her of her magical gifts.

"I'm a mess," Bloom groaned. "I was unable to use my power when I needed it most, and now the whole Magic Dimension is in serious jeopardy. I've got to *do* something!" She stood and picked up Kiko, hugging the soft bunny. "But what? I mean . . . I've lost my powers. I'm not a fairy. I'm not *anything* anymore."

Bloom's phone rang, and Stella picked it up.

It was Prince Sky.

Sky was standing outside Redfountain, the school for young wizards known as Specialists, leaning against a tall orange building. Other young Specialists milled around in the courtyard close by. Sky had chosen the spot so he could talk privately.

"Hi, uh . . . Stella, may I speak to Bloom?" Sky asked. He flicked up his blond bangs nervously. He paused for a moment. "Of course, no problem. I'll wait."

After a second of muffled conversation on the other end, Stella returned to the phone with bad news.

"She can't?" asked Sky. He sighed. Bloom wouldn't talk to him. And why should she? He wouldn't be surprised if she never talked to him again. He needed to explain to her that his family had arranged his engagement to Princess Diaspro . . . and that he didn't want to marry her. In fact, he'd tried to break up with Diaspro!

Sky hung up his phone and ran off, not wanting the other guys to see how upset he was.

But Prince Sky hadn't noticed that someone had overheard his conversation. His friend Riven had been kneeling nearby, pretending to pull something out of his book bag.

Riven was more of a frenemy to Sky than a true friend. The purple-haired teenage wizard had made a secret deal with the Trix to spy on his fellow Redfountain students and to report on anything that had to do with Bloom.

Riven chuckled nastily. "Rejected by his little fairy," he muttered. "Darcy will be happy to hear this."

He wasted no time before sneaking away from Redfountain. On his flashy windrider hovercycle, he zoomed through the forest and blasted up the winding elevated road to the witches' college, Cloudtower.

When Riven reached the school, he was surprised to hear a voice calling him from Miss Griffin's tower office. "Riven!" Darcy hailed him from the high window. "Over here!"

Riven made a sharp turn, looped around, and landed his windrider on the wide ledge. Then he pulled off his helmet, gracefully leapt through the window, and strode into the dark, cluttered office.

He raised a sharp eyebrow when he saw Icy sitting

in Miss Griffin's chair and Stormy perched on the headmistress's big desk. "What are you doing in here?" he asked. "Since when does Griffin let you use her office?"

Darcy slunk around behind him. "Since we took it from her," she replied. The window shades slammed closed, blocking Riven from his windrider.

"What do you mean?" Riven demanded, clenching his hands into fists and stepping back in alarm.

Instead of answering him, the Trix simply cackled with evil glee.

Chapter 3

Riven glared at Stormy and Icy. "Where's Griffin?" he insisted. "What have you done?"

Icy smiled as she stood up lazily and sauntered over to stand by Stormy's side. "Oh," she said, her eyes filling with red light, "we just put her in her place."

Behind him, Riven could feel frighteningly forceful magical energies gathering. He wheeled around to see Darcy floating off the floor, her long, thick brown hair blowing out behind her, her eyes blank white and glowing with power.

"And now we're going to put you in *yours*," hissed Darcy.

Cackling as they floated in midair, the three

witches circled Riven, swirling magic around him. They spun faster and faster, until they were almost a blur.

"What?" Riven cried. He whirled around, trying to focus on the spinning witches. "Stop that!"

"Oh, Riven," Darcy taunted. "Did you think we cared?"

Icy and Stormy joined Darcy in mocking laughter, revolving even faster around the confused, handsome Specialist.

"No!" Riven replied, but his voice revealed that he *had* thought they'd liked him, maybe a little. Furious, he pulled out his jeweled energy sword pommel and activated his blade of cold purple light. "You tricked me!" he growled. "Curses on you!"

The Trix howled with glee, thrilled with their evil betrayal.

Then Darcy pulled back her arm and conjured the same spell Miss Griffin had tried on the Trix in the dining tower. "Sphere of Oblivion!" she intoned, and a sizzling purple ball appeared in her hand. She hurled the sphere at Riven and it slammed into the floor at his feet.

A sinister black disk spread out from where the sphere had struck. It wasn't just dark—it was nothingness, a *void*. The disk quickly grew into a dome, surrounding Riven with chilly, echoing emptiness.

Riven seemed to shrink as the witches grew to three times his size, hovering over him and laughing. He gasped in fear as they raised their hands to him, each palm glowing with blinding white light.

The light seared into Riven and he lost consciousness.

After getting rid of Riven, Darcy dissipated the Sphere of Oblivion. The three Trix grasped hands, and as they concentrated, wriggling purple magic symbols began to squiggle around them, shimmering with energy. Hovering cross-legged in the air, they formed a tight triangle and closed their eyes, focusing on making their magical connection as powerful as possible, strengthening the writhing purple plasma that surrounded them.

"The Dragon Flame that we have sought for so

long is now ours," said Icy in a deep voice. "We will begin our conquest with Redfountain, and then . . . the whole Magix World!"

"At last," Stormy breathed.

Icy opened her eyes and narrowed them at the other witch. "Let's not be rash, Stormy," she scolded. As she spoke, the purple plasma streaked away toward the top of the tower. "First we must raise our army . . . the Creatures of the Dark!"

The Trix giggled nastily as the streaks of plasma spiraled up into the moody clouds that always hung over Cloudtower. Jagged purple lightning flashed, and a thick, steaming rain started to fall.

When the weird rain reached the grassy fields around the school's central mountain, the ground began to bubble and boil with purple muck, forming into thousands of churning puddles.

"Rise up, Creatures of the Dark!" Icy shouted from the headmistress's office in the tallest tower. "As your rulers, we command it!"

Out of each puddle crawled a vile, monstrous purple *thing*. At first, the things all looked like soggy centipedes, but then they mutated, some growing bat wings, some developing vicious pincers and claws and fangs, some turning into hulking armored beasts or toxic worms wriggling in roiling heaps.

Now the Trix had a grotesque, fiendish army under their control.

The flying creatures flapped up to the tower and circled it, their hideous cries echoing in the pouring rain, while below, the creeping monsters gathered around the castle, awaiting further orders from the wicked Trix.

Inside a lower school corridor, a fuzzy ogre named Knut stopped short when he saw that the other end of the hall was writhing with disgusting beings. "Ugh," he said, wrinkling his nose. "Time to get out of here!"

Knut had worked as a caretaker in Cloudtower his whole life and knew its layout and its secrets better than anyone. He quickly escaped the castle through a back exit and hurried through the deep forest toward Redfountain.

Once he reached the wizards' school, Knut

rushed up to the office of Mr. Saladin, Redfountain's headmaster.

Mr. Saladin's office was filled with mystical objects and shifting shadows. The ancient wizard, who had long white hair, stood in front of his lavish desk waiting for Knut, his tall staff of power firmly in his grip.

"What are you doing here, Knut?" Mr. Saladin asked suspiciously. "Spying for the Trix?"

Knut froze in the middle of the vast office. He was a brutish ogre, and he had done mean things while following orders, like attacking Bloom in Gardenia, but he wasn't really a wicked monster. "Oh, no, Mr. Saladin," he said. "I had to get away from them! They're not just bad anymore." His voice lowered to a whisper. "They're . . . evil."

A burst of purple light behind him made Knut whirl around. He grimaced when he saw flickering holograms of the three Trix behind him. They did not look happy.

"There you are, Knut," Icy snarled. "You traitor."

Her projection sneered at him. "Do you think Saladin can keep you safe?"

The three witches burst into vicious giggles.

"Well," said Darcy, "you'll be sorry you ran out on us." She pointed a sharp-nailed finger at Knut. "We're going to destroy Redfountain down to the ground."

Mr. Saladin was in no mood for the Trix's bullying. He lurched forward and thrust his dragon-headed, jeweled wooden staff at the holograms. "You crazy witches!" he shouted, and fired a bolt of spluttering lightning, banishing the projections in a bright flash.

With the Trix's holograms gone, Mr. Saladin and Knut stared worriedly at the empty place where the sisters had been threatening Redfountain a second before.

Knut sighed glumly. "They'll be back," he said.

Chapter 4

Headmaster Saladin and Knut rushed out of the office and warned the students and instructors at Redfountain about the upcoming siege on the school. Everyone assembled in the courtyard for further instruction, lined up in military rows in tight squads.

With his top teacher, brawny Mr. Codatorta, at his side, Mr. Saladin hobbled to the front of the ranks of the Specialists and faced the crowd. "Young men!" he announced. "Soon we will be under attack by the Trix and their evil army. The time has come . . . to do battle!"

"Are you ready?" Mr. Codatorta called out.

Prince Sky stood with his best friends, Timmy

and Brandon, in front of their squad of Specialists. They all raised their fists in the air.

"We're ready!" replied cute, bespectacled Timmy.

Mr. Saladin nodded. "We must fight with everything that is in us," he said.

Then the witches' boiling storm reached Redfountain, darkening the sky overhead. Purple lightning split the clouds, and gooey black rain poured down over the wizards' school.

In the Redfountain courtyard, wherever the rain hit the ground, purple puddles bubbled and churned. As the young wizards watched with worry creasing their faces, hundreds of grubby centipedes climbed out of the oozing puddles. Clacking and chattering, the horrible beings advanced toward the cringing Specialists.

Some of the creatures glommed together in big piles to form larger beasts with sharp spiked claws and thick armored carapaces. Wriggling tentacles protruded from their jaws.

"This is it," Mr. Codatorta declared. "The time has

come." Raising his arm to point at the monsters, he ordered his teenage troops, "Take up your positions!"

Groups of Specialists activated their energy swords and rushed forward to engage the beasts in battle. They used all their skills and training to dodge the monsters' swiping pincers, keeping them back with their blazing swords. But there were too many creatures, and they began to overwhelm the forces in the courtyard.

Dark-haired Brandon and Prince Sky charged into the melee, attacking with their swords. Timmy stayed behind for a second to pull out his starlight blaster, his eyes wide with alarm. "They just keep coming!" he cried, firing the weapon at the monsters.

Diamond-shaped shards of energy swirled out of the blaster and sizzled one of the biggest beasts, tearing it apart in chunks of purple goo. Timmy smiled but quickly looked worried again when all the goo from the fallen monster rapidly collected on the ground. It boiled up again, rebuilding itself even bigger than before.

"Oh, no!" Timmy gasped as the monster snagged him around the neck with a massive claw and hoisted him into the air. He struggled, kicking his legs, but he couldn't free himself from its strong grip. The beast grasped Timmy's face with its tentacles, preparing to finish him off.

Knut charged the horrible creature and thumped him hard on his shell with his meaty fists. The beast dropped Timmy, who fell to the ground and rolled away. Then Knut hefted the monster over his head and hurled it across the courtyard, knocking down two other beasts.

"Thanks, Knut," said Timmy, climbing to his feet, and the ogre bared his big teeth in a wide grin.

At the top of the courtyard stairs, Headmaster Saladin raised his dragon-headed staff in the air. He shouted words in a mystical language as his body and the staff became outlined in white light. Then a flash burst out of the mouth of the dragonhead and soared upward, expanding into a wide blast as it reached the storm clouds above Redfountain. The clouds lightened, and the dark, viscous rain stopped falling.

Mr. Saladin wasn't done. He intoned more magical phrases, raised his hand, and conjured a yellow power spiral that spun in tight circles toward the monsters in the courtyard. "Go away, creatures of evil!" Mr. Saladin boomed. "Depart from Redfountain!"

Any creature the yellow spiral touched quickly dissolved into a smoking heap of purple goo. In moments, all the beasts had been reduced to squirming puddles.

Headmaster Saladin heaved a heavy sigh of relief.

But he had relaxed too soon. The purple puddles churned and spewed out more giant creatures, which howled in fury.

The exhausted Specialists were just getting ready to attack the reborn beasts when the Trix appeared, floating over Redfountain with lightning streaking across the clouds behind them. The witches laughed, enjoying themselves.

"Newsflash, old man," Icy sneered at Headmaster Saladin. "Redfountain is history!" She held out her hands and concentrated on creating a beam of pure frozen power. The beam twisted out of her palms, turning into a shrieking dragon of intense cold that soared toward Redfountain's main building. The ice dragon wrapped its long, sinuous body around the school's spire three times, settling in loops around the structure. Then it turned to solid ice, encasing the school in jagged frozen crystals.

A crack zigged through the top third of the ice and the peak split off, taking the top spire with it. The spire slid down to smash into chunks outside the school walls.

Mr. Codatorta gasped in horror at the destruction of Redfountain's tower. "Strategic withdrawal!" he hollered to the student Specialists. "Everyone to their battleships!"

The Trix, giggling, teleported back to Cloudtower.

Meanwhile, the student wizards hurried to board their escape vessels while the frozen walls of the school continued to crumble around them. One by one, their aerodynamic ships rocketed over the forests around Redfountain and safely into the sky.

Headmaster Saladin gave one last, sad look down

at the ruins of his school before his ship carried him out of sight.

Icy, Darcy, and Stormy continued laughing as they gathered around Miss Griffin's desk back at Cloudtower. They had redecorated the office, and now a crystal ball and a thick magical book sat on the desk.

"Weren't we just great?" cheered Darcy. "We totally sent them flying." She gave Stormy several high fives in a row.

"We rule," Stormy agreed.

Icy slumped down in Miss Griffin's chair, tapping her fingertips in front of her face. "Ah, but we're not done yet, sisters," she said. An evil glint gleamed in her blue eyes. "The best is yet to come."

The wizards landed their spacecraft in the Alfea College courtyard. Disembarking quickly,

Headmaster Saladin and Mr. Codatorta led their battle-weary students toward the main entrance to the fairies' school.

"Alfea hasn't yet come under attack," Mr. Codatorta told Saladin as they marched up the wide stairs. "We'll be able to reorganize our troops here."

The doors to the school opened magically, and the tired teenagers filed into the entrance hall, where they were welcomed by Miss Faragonda.

"Come on in, young men," Headmistress Faragonda said kindly. "We'll help you get settled."

Mr. Saladin approached the headmistress with Mr. Codatorta. "Thank you, Faragonda," he said. "The situation is critical." The old wizard bowed his head sadly, his bushy white eyebrows drooping. "Redfountain has been destroyed."

Miss Faragonda closed her eyes and shook her head in sympathy. "I am so sorry, Saladin," she said. Then she looked up and raised a finger in warning. "But I fear this is only the beginning!"

Chapter 5

In a cold dungeon, high in one of Cloudtower's tall spires, Riven woke up. He was unsure how long he had been unconscious. He found himself imprisoned in a murky cell strewn with piles of grubby straw. Riven groaned, his body aching from the Trix's violent magic.

"Hey, kiddo!" a voice hissed from across the corridor.

"Huh?" Riven muttered. Struggling to his feet, he limped over to the barred door to his cell and peeked through the narrow window into the hall.

Riven could see a pale older witch in the window of the door opposite his, peering out into the darkness from her own cell.

"Miss Griffin!" Riven said. "Is that you? What are you doing here?"

"Paying the price for my arrogance," Miss Griffin replied. She looked down dejectedly. "I should have seen earlier that the Trix were truly dangerous."

Riven raised his sharp eyebrows. "It's not your fault," he said. "No one knew what they were planning." After being betrayed by the Trix, Riven could barely remember why he had trusted them in the first place. It had seemed exciting to collaborate with the witches, and they had pretended to be impressed by him. Riven had loved the attention after living for so long in Prince Sky's shadow. "Especially me," he sighed.

Still, Riven had never been a quitter. He inspected the lock on his door and noticed that its keyhole was a funny T shape. Then he spotted a tiny bit of twisted wire on the dirty floor and he snatched it up, starting to hope.

"But," he began, "maybe I can get us out of here." It only took a few seconds of fiddling with the wire in the lock before it sprang open. Now, that was a skill nobody had taught him in wizard school! While Riven's rough childhood had made him tough and snarky, the skills he'd learned growing up on his own came in awfully handy on occasion. He would've liked to see pampered Prince Sky try to pick a lock sometime!

Riven pushed open the door and hurried over to the headmistress's cell door. "Don't worry, Miss Griffin," he told her. "I'll get you out of here in a second." He kneeled down to work his lockpicking skills on her door.

"Don't waste your time, kid," Miss Griffin said.

"Huh?" Riven muttered, glancing up in surprise.

Miss Griffin smiled at him from behind the bars in the window. "Believe me, if it were as easy as that," she said, nodding at the wire in his hand, "my powers would have taken care of that lock long before now." She turned around and smiled at a group of teen witches in the cell with her. The students were hard at work, brewing up a magical potion with a mop and wooden bucket. "But," Miss Griffin said, "we may still find a way."

A scuttling sound made Riven turn quickly and peer down the dark corridor. "What is that?" he asked, alarmed.

"Creatures of the Dark!" Miss Griffin answered with fear in her voice. "Save yourself!"

Riven wasn't just going to leave the headmistress locked up. "But—"

"Run!" Miss Griffin cried.

"But you—"

Miss Griffin shook her head firmly. "You can do nothing for me."

Hundreds of horrible purple things with many legs lurched out of the darkness and scrambled down the hall toward Riven.

"Run!" shrieked Miss Griffin.

Riven bolted down the corridor with the awful creatures in hot pursuit. He glanced back and saw that behind the little centipedes, a towering purple beast with sharp claws and a head dripping with tentacles was stomping down the hall. After that, he didn't look back again. He just sprinted as fast as he could.

The monsters chased Riven up a steep flight of stairs and through a long passageway with a high arched ceiling and guttering torches along the walls. Riven made a sharp turn at the next corner . . . and found himself in a narrow hall. The only exit was a peaked window at one end. "Oh, no," he panted. "No!"

He turned around and saw the creepy creatures crawling toward him, blocking his escape from that end.

"Looks like this is the only way out," Riven said decisively, and he raced toward the window. Stepping through it, he discovered a narrow terrace far above the ground. The view was dizzying—all of the land of Magix seemed spread out before him.

Riven glanced back, but the hall was filled with monsters.

He was out of options.

"Well, here goes nothing," he said, and jumped off the terrace.

His cape fluttering behind him, Riven plummeted down the length of the tower, falling face-first toward the spiky buildings below, screaming in complete terror.

CHAPTER 6

Prince Sky was standing next to Bloom in Headmistress Faragonda's office when he was struck with a sharp sensation of sheer fear. "Riven," he mumbled, pressing the heel of his palm to his forehead. It felt like a psychic cry for help from his friend.

"What's the matter?" Bloom asked.

Sky shook off the jolt of panic. "Nothing," he replied. "I just got this strange feeling." He didn't want to worry Bloom about Riven just then. They had more immediate troubles to handle. And Riven was tough and usually could take care of himself.

Bloom nodded as she returned her attention to

the adults in front of Miss Faragonda's desk. The headmistress stood in the middle of a line formed by Knut, Mr. Codatorta, Mr. Saladin, and a tiny pixie-like teacher. Standing beside Bloom and Sky were Brandon and Stella.

"Bloom," said Miss Faragonda, "I think your plan makes sense."

Sky turned to face Bloom, his blond eyebrows knitted with concern. "Come on!" he argued heatedly, his protective side making his voice angrier than he intended. Bloom didn't even have her magical powers anymore! "Only a total lunatic would go anywhere near Cloudtower right now."

"But I have to get my Dragon Flame back," Bloom replied, "and I'm sure it's in Cloudtower. Besides, it's the last thing the Trix would expect."

Brandon crossed his arms. "And how are you planning to get in?"

"Easy," grunted Knut. "We can take the tunnels."

"There are ancient tunnels linking all three schools," Bloom explained, "and Knut can lead the way." She pressed her hand to her chest. "Look, I'm going. With you or without you."

Stella held Bloom's shoulder. "Not without me!" she said cheerfully.

Bloom smiled warmly at her faithful friend. From the first moment she'd met Stella, she knew she had found someone who would always have her back. Bloom would always help Stella, too, no matter how scary the crisis. They were both Winx fairies, after all! With Stella's sunny powers on her side, Bloom was certain she could recover her Dragon Flame from those awful Trix.

Miss Faragonda nodded and stepped forward to speak to Bloom. "You must leave immediately," the headmistress instructed. She gestured toward the huge picture window in her office. Heavy, threatening storm clouds were gathering over the lake at the outskirts of Alfea. Those clouds were leaden with the gooey magical rain that could spawn another army of dreadfully creepy creatures. Nobody wanted to think about how long the fairies could hold out against an invasion, even with help from the Specialists.

"The final attack is coming," said Miss Faragonda. "Please hurry."

After quickly gathering a few supplies, Bloom, Sky, Stella, and Brandon followed Knut to a hatch in Alfea's basement. Below the hatch was a deep, narrow tunnel, and the students and Knut climbed down a long, shaky ladder to reach the complex maze below.

Outside the first small, damp room were several branches leading in different directions. Knut held up his torch and peered down the dark tunnels with a confused look on his brutish face.

The Specialists stepped up behind him, each of them holding their energy swords at the ready. Sky's blade was blue, while Brandon's glowed with bright green light.

"Well, Knut," asked Sky, "which way do we go to get to Cloudtower?"

"I'm not sure," Knut admitted, rubbing his chin.

"Everything looks different down here."

But then, suddenly seeming certain, Knut chose a direction and stomped forward. With no other choice, the teenagers followed him. The ogre led them along narrow passageways and under dripping pipes, through stone archways and down steep steps, barely avoiding hidden dangers like unstable piles of rubble and concealed pitfalls. Finally, they reached a muddy, circular room with three exits, all of which looked exactly the same.

Stella hurried to catch up to Knut, her blue fairy wings fluttering on her back. "There are three tunnels," she said. "Which one do we take?"

"Um . . . ," moaned Knut. "I don't know."

"What?" Stella gasped. She was completely fed up with the ogre's lack of leadership . . . and she hated being so far underground with no access to the open air, which made her feel terribly claustrophobic. "In the last half hour alone, you've nearly led us into fourteen death traps!"

"Stella," Bloom said gently, "Knut is doing his

best." She touched the strap of Knut's overalls and looked up into his red eyes. "Knut . . . you have a great sense of smell," she reminded him. "Use it!"

Knut nodded and inhaled deeply, sniffing the foul air in the subterranean tunnels. After wriggling his nose for a while, he pointed his torch at the center entranceway ahead of them. "It's this one," he declared.

The group followed Knut into the new passage, which had dark brown rock walls and seemed ominously quiet and creepy in the flickering light of the ogre's torch. The students peered around nervously as Knut strode confidently down the tunnel.

"Are you sure?" asked Stella.

"If I say it's this one," Knut replied, "then this one it is!"

Chapter 7

Seconds after Knut declared how sure he was that they were going the right way, the group wandered into a nest of the most slimy, disgusting sewer monsters imaginable. The creatures were blobs the color of dried blood, with bulbous eyes on stalks and gaping mouths filled with dripping fangs. They were big, too—three times the size of Knut.

Nobody wanted to fight those repulsive, giant slug-things. They even smelled like rotten snot. The teenagers and the ogre just turned and ran back down the tunnel, screaming.

The gross monsters chased them, oozing slime all over everything and gibbering in mindless grunts.

After racing blindly through the tunnels, Bloom, Stella, Brandon, Sky, and Knut finally took enough twists and turns that they lost the creatures. They rested for a moment. They couldn't hear the awful noises any longer, but they also had no idea where they were.

Back in the lead, Knut found a small chamber with a ladder that ended at a hatch on the ceiling. Hoping it was an exit, the ogre climbed the ladder and pushed the hatch open.

Instantly, dirty water flooded into the room. The group was whooshed back into the tunnel, tumbling in the rushing water. They had to climb a wall of crumbling rock to escape the churning stream. Working together, they hoisted Knut up after them.

Then they stumbled into a cave where sticky vines grabbed their arms and legs. Knut had to rip the vines apart with his bare hands, and Sky and Brandon sliced the tangling plants with their swords so the group could escape.

After a few minutes, they reached a cavern that

seemed safe, with sheer rock walls and a dirt floor covered with reddish mounds. Bloom sat down on one of the mounds, which was surprisingly soft and comfortable, and Stella perched beside her.

"I'm exhausted!" said Stella, and the boys gasped heavily alongside her, trying to catch their breath. When Knut sat down on a mound, it began to wriggle under him! The ogre leapt up as the pile of dirt broke open, revealing an enormous grub inside. Again they were on a run for their lives!

Finally, they stopped in a damp, dripping, but empty tunnel, all of them panting desperately.

After Stella had rested a moment, she pointed a finger angrily at Knut. "Oh yeah, we'll get out of here, no problem," she said to him sarcastically. "Right!"

"It's not my fault," Knut protested. "This place is full of smells." Then he caught a whiff of something that seemed familiar, and he inhaled deeply. "Hang on a second," he said. "I know that stink."

Knut followed his nose to the wall and leaned against it with one of his huge hands.

The wall cracked open, and Knut tumbled through the gaping hole. With a scream, he slid down a long chute into the darkness.

"It's Cloudtower!" the ogre bellowed from far below.

Bracing themselves against the smell, the teenagers shuffled down the chute to meet Knut at the bottom. They were in a large, filthy room full of piles of moldy trash and broken furniture.

"It's Cloudtower's garbage dump," said Bloom.

Stella pinched her nostrils shut to avoid breathing the putrid fumes in the room. "Yuck!" she exclaimed. "What a stench!"

Bloom strode over to the ogre, who was stuck in a pile of muck. "Let's give Knut a hand," she said. "Come on."

The four students were pulling Knut out of the filth on the floor when Bloom heard something move on the other side of the room.

"What was that?" she asked, her eyes wide with worry.

Stella yanked on Knut's arm. "I don't know and I don't want to know," she grumbled. Her sunny disposition had really dimmed underground!

The greenish slime on the ground suddenly began to bubble and rise. Each bubble burst, revealing huge beetle-like insects that quickly surrounded the teenagers and the ogre.

"Uh-oh," Knut groaned.

"What are those things?" Stella cried as the creatures scuttled closer.

"Dump roaches—giant garbage-eating bugs!" Knut replied.

"Eww," whimpered Stella. "Disgusting!"

Sky raised his blue energy sword. "Knut!" he called. "Will they attack us?"

One of the dump roaches flung out a spiky leg and snagged Knut's foot with it, dragging the ogre closer and then dangling him upside down.

"Yeah!" Knut answered Sky.

The huge bug lowered Knut toward its gaping, sharp jaws, and the ogre howled in panic.

Before the Specialists could even move, Bloom leapt up and bashed the giant roach on the leg with a twisted pipe she'd found. The creature dropped Knut and backed away.

"For a fairy with no powers," Knut told Bloom, "you sure pack a punch!"

"Thanks," Bloom said with a smile. Then she gasped as she saw the biggest roach yet, a fat red one with an almost human head, looming behind Sky. "Look out!" she cried. "Sky!"

Her warning came too late. The gigantic insect grabbed Sky in its pincers and tossed him to the dirty ground, knocking his sword out of his hand.

Sky tried to crawl away, but the massive bug pushed him down again. It opened its mouth to take a bite of Sky's leg.

Before it could close its jaws, someone leapt onto the creature's vast back. The insect bucked and twisted, forgetting about Sky, trying to dislodge the hooded figure on top of it.

"Yeehaw!" came a guy's voice. He rode the bug

like a bronco. When the insect paused for a moment, he pulled out a starlight blaster and aimed it at the creature's head. "Your number's up!" he cried, firing the weapon.

The shot hurt the gargantuan bug enough that it flung the mystery man off its back and raced away on its many legs.

"Guys, look!" Stella called, pointing at the retreating dump roaches. "They're all going away!"

The guy who had saved Sky stood up. His face was hidden by the hood of his robe, which seemed to be made of patched-together rags. "That's right," he said. "The one I zapped was the leader."

"Hey," Sky said, "um . . . who are you, anyway?"

"What?" the guy asked, turning to face Sky. "You don't recognize your old friend anymore?" He opened his robe and dropped it down his back, revealing a familiar Specialist uniform . . . and a head covered with spikes of vibrant purple hair.

Sky and Brandon shouted in unison, "Riven!"

CHAPTER 8

Now that Knut had found the garbage dump, he was much more certain of the path through the tunnels into Cloudtower. Holding his torch, the ogre led the group out of the dump and through dark stone passageways that slowly wound upward.

As they walked, Sky quizzed Riven about what he'd been up to. "What in the world were you doing in Cloudtower's garbage dump?" he asked.

Wincing, Riven replied, "Darcy turned on me. I was trying to escape the dungeon the Trix locked me in, and I jumped out a high window to get away from these horrible creatures of darkness. I thought I was doomed, but as I fell, I hit the side of Cloudtower's dome and slid safely down . . . although I landed in the garbage dump."

Riven paused and scratched the side of his purple hair before continuing. "You guys," he said sincerely, "I'm sorry for how I acted. For all the stuff I did."

With a smile, Sky threw his arm around Riven's shoulders. "It's okay," he said. "I'm glad to have you back."

Up at the front of the line, Bloom turned around. "Knut has finally found the way into Cloudtower!" she called cheerfully.

The group hurried onward, excited to finally be leaving the dark tunnels behind.

High above, in Miss Griffin's office atop Cloudtower's tallest tower, Icy sat cross-legged on the headmistress's desk. She looked a little glum as she pored over battle plans, trying to figure out the best time to attack Alfea with her grotesque army of darkness.

A big green beetle scurried into the office. It stopped in front of the desk, and its back carapace opened up to reveal a huge, glistening eyeball.

Icy peered down at the eyeball, which acted as a crystal ball. It showed her an image that made her smile: Knut, Sky, Brandon, Riven, Stella, and Bloom walking through the corridors under Cloudtower.

"Oh, look," she cooed. "It's our little friends. I wondered when they would show up."

Hopping off the desk, Icy summoned Darcy and Stormy. "Sisters!" she called. "We have guests!" Her eyes narrowed menacingly. "Let's go say hello."

Underneath Cloudtower, Knut finally led the teens out of the stone tunnels and into corridors with green walls and purple pillars, like the rest of Cloudtower. "Here we are!" Knut cheered. He pointed down a hall that led to the gloomy dungeons. "And that's where the Trix hide all their secrets."

"Been there, done that," Riven joked. He nudged

Brandon's shoulder. "Let's see if we can find Miss Griffin."

Hoisting his glowing green energy sword onto his shoulder, Brandon followed Riven toward the dungeon cells. "Back soon!" he called to the others.

"We'll catch up with you in a minute," Sky told the other Specialists, and then he, Stella, Bloom, and Knut headed in the other direction, where the ogre thought the Trix might hide something they didn't want anyone to find.

They trooped through angular halls. Weird ratbirds flapped along the ceiling rafters. Eventually, they reached an ornate orange door, which opened as they approached.

"It must be in here," Bloom said, hurrying into the chamber. It was a circular room glowing with orange light. All around the edges were eerie stone statues of witches performing incantations. On a dais in the middle was a big, shining brazier flickering with bright flames.

"My Dragon Flame!" Bloom cheered. "I've found

it!" She hurried onto the dais, closer to the fire, but before she could reach it, the flames suddenly turned to cold blue ice.

Behind Sky, Stella, and Knut, the three Trix sauntered into the chamber.

"Surprise!" taunted Icy. "That's not your Dragon Flame, Bloom." She glared at the fairy and raised her hands to attack with her frozen magic.

Bloom winced, anticipating the assault, but she was shocked when an explosion of green energy blasted the Trix instead.

Icy, Stormy, and Darcy were blown off their feet and thrown violently against the chamber wall, where they left dents in the stonework before tumbling hard to the floor.

In the chamber doorway stood Miss Griffin, blazing with furious power. Her hands glowed with bright green light, and her whole body was outlined with mystical energy. Her eyes shone with blistering green wrath.

"Good evening, girls," Miss Griffin said, striding into the chamber.

Icy sat up on the floor, her bad attitude intact. "So . . . you managed to escape, Miss Griffin." She stood as her headmistress began to wave her arms in preparation for a magic spell. "What do you think you're doing?" demanded Icy.

Miss Griffin finished her spell, and a brilliant wall of shimmering purple light appeared, trapping the Trix against the chamber wall. Then the headmistress whirled around to face Bloom, Stella, Sky, and Knut. "Run, you fools!" she hissed.

They didn't need to be told twice. Everyone sprinted out of the chamber, meeting up with Riven, Brandon, and a group of hooded student witches in the corridor.

Miss Griffin stopped just outside the chamber. She grunted as she conjured another spell, sealing up the room with dozens of spiky tongues of rough rock. Then she ran after the others, crying, "Hurry! To the Windswept Terrace!"

Inside the chamber, Icy shook with rage. "No!" she screamed. Her frosty powers exploded around her, cracking Miss Griffin's purple energy wall, which crumbled into shards at her feet.

But the Trix witches were still trapped by the sharp spikes of stone blocking the door.

"How are we going to get out of here?" Stormy asked.

Icy glared at the rock formations the headmistress had created. "You think a little granite is going to stop me?" she sneered. "Step aside, sisters."

Stormy and Darcy moved out of the way, and Icy trembled as she called up her powers with a deep cry of effort.

Huge green beams of intense energy shot from her hands at the rocks, blasting them to dust and leaving shallow craters on the floor.

Icy had cleared the doorway. The evil witches were free!

Bloom is the fairy with the power of Dragon Flame—until it is stolen from her! But she is determined to get her magic back.

Stormy, Icy, and Darcy are three evil witches who call themselves the Trix. They steal Bloom's Dragon Flame and plot to take over the magical universe!

Cloudtower is a school for witches. It is where the Trix begin their conquest of the planet Magix.

Miss Griffin is the headmistress of Cloudtower—until she is forced to flee the Trix.

The Specialists are trained in combat—but they are no match for the Trix!

Stormy uses her
powers to conjure up
dangerous storms!

Icy can freeze her
enemies in their tracks.

In the final showdown with the Trix, Bloom discovers that she never really lost the power of Dragon Flame.

CHAPTER 9

The Windswept Terrace could only be reached by a long, winding stone staircase along the outside of Cloudtower. The wind was fierce so high up, with powerful gusts threatening to blow the students to their doom.

Led by Miss Griffin, dozens of student witches hurried up the steps, huddling in their robes and hoods, careful to stay as close to the wall as possible as they climbed.

Following the many witches up the treacherous staircase were Bloom, Stella, Sky, Riven, and Brandon, along with Knut, who protected the rear of the line of escapees.

When everyone had made it up to the Windswept Terrace, they clustered together on the high platform, forming a circle around Miss Griffin.

"Those barriers won't hold the Trix for long!" Miss Griffin shouted over the howling winds, unaware that the three evil witches had already escaped. "I'll conjure up a dimensional portal to Alfea."

She swirled the winds around her and raised her hands to summon bolts of lightning in the dark clouds above. The storm howled and began to circle an opening in the atmosphere. A green cone of light shone down onto the Windswept Terrace. The portal was open!

One by one, their robes flapping in the wind, the witches floated into the cone of light and through the opening in the clouds, where they were transported to Alfea.

As more and more witches escaped Cloudtower safely, the strain of holding the portal open began to show on Miss Griffin's face. "We must escape!" she cried. "The Creatures of the Dark are coming!"

Bloom peered over the edge of the platform and

saw a horde of purple armored beasts. Their sharp claws clacked as they climbed up the long, curving staircase to the terrace.

"Miss Griffin!" shouted Sky. "Get everyone out! I'll create a diversion."

The headmistress nodded. "Use this!" she said, and she quickly conjured up a tricked-out blue windrider.

As Sky mounted the magical windrider hovercycle, bands of armor encircled his legs. A sturdy helmet with a glowing red visor materialized on his head. Sky looked breathtakingly cool in his new gear.

Bloom cried, "I'm coming with you!" She hopped onto the windrider, and a helmet and armor similar to his encased her body.

Sky took off, and Bloom wrapped her arms tightly around his trim waist while the windrider soared upward, zooming away just as the purple beasts breached the terrace.

Riven stepped into the portal's cone of light. "Good luck with that," he called to his friends.

"Bloom!" Stella shouted. "Be careful!" Then she, too, rose into the green energy cone.

Miss Griffin was the last person on the terrace. She was concentrating on maintaining the portal long enough for Stella and Riven to escape, but the horrible monsters were barreling right toward her.

Sky swooped down on his windrider and bashed into the beasts, knocking them off the terrace. He hoped that would give Miss Griffin enough time to complete her spell.

Finally, all the students were safe, and Miss Griffin leapt into the cone herself. She floated up and called to Sky and Bloom, "Get out of here, you two!"

Bloom watched as Miss Griffin vanished into the portal, and then she hugged Sky more tightly around his waist. "That's everyone!" she cheered.

"Time to go!" Sky yelled, and he gunned the windrider, smashing into more beasts as he blasted off the terrace into the open air. He rocketed the windrider back toward Cloudtower and zoomed down a winding ramp to the ground. Then, with Bloom clinging to him, Sky whooshed along a forested road away from the infested witches' school.

Angry lightning zigged and zagged in the dark storm clouds as Sky steered the windrider deeper into the forest toward Alfea.

"We're almost there, Bloom!" Sky hollered . . . just as he spotted familiar ugly beasts blocking the road ahead.

Sky jackknifed the windrider, gaining speed and altitude. "Monsters!" he groaned. "Hang on! I'm going to try to lose them!"

Bloom ducked her helmet against Sky's back as he steered the windrider wildly, maneuvering around exploding energy beams blasting out of the beasts' eyes. One of the beams detonated too close, and the back of the windrider began to spit dark smoke. Bloom twisted her head to check out the damage. "Sky!" she cried. "We're hit!"

The windrider fishtailed, careening out of control. It spun around at top speed and bashed through a guardrail over a cliff, trailing smoke as it plummeted toward the trees far below.

Bloom screamed as Sky wrestled with the

windrider's controls. He managed to skim the tops of the trees, barely avoiding collision; then he steered the flailing craft along a ravine and into a clearing in the forest, where he made a rough, bouncy landing in the overgrown grass.

Outside in the pretty courtyard of Alfea College, Miss Faragonda, Mr. Saladin, and Mr. Codatorta were overseeing military drills of the Specialists and fairies, preparing for the attack by the Trix and their creatures of darkness. Suddenly Flora, Musa, and Tecna appeared, running across the courtyard toward the headmistress.

"Miss Faragonda!" called Flora urgently. "Miss Faragonda!" She reached the headmistress and panted for a second, catching her breath. "We've detected a temporal distortion!"

Musa pointed across the courtyard. "Over there," she said. "Right next to the well!"

A brilliant light flashed in an open area in front of the school, and a group of people materialized, glimmering for a moment before solidifying.

"It's Griffin and her students!" said Miss Faragonda. "What a relief!"

Not only had Miss Griffin and her teenage witches arrived safely, but so had Stella, Riven, and Knut.

Miss Faragonda strode over, her hands clasped behind her back, and met Miss Griffin on a flagstone path. "Welcome to Alfea, Griffin," the headmistress said warmly. "I see that your students have followed you."

"Yes," Miss Griffin replied, smiling. "But it is thanks to *your* students that we were able to escape from the clutches of those three power-crazed witches."

Flora, Musa, and Tecna rushed over to greet Stella, thrilled that their beloved friend and sister Winx was safe.

"Where's Bloom?" asked Flora, holding Stella's hands.

"She was with Sky," Stella replied. She ducked her head in worry. "She should be back by now. . . ."

Chapter 10

In the clearing somewhere deep in the dense woods between Cloudtower and Alfea, Sky lay on his back under his windrider, fiddling with the broken parts in a hatch in the undercarriage.

Finally, he gave up and rolled up to his knees. "Well," he told Bloom, "it's totally busted." He climbed to his feet dejectedly.

"So . . . ," Bloom replied, "I guess that means we're walking."

"Looks like it," Sky said, dusting off his snazzy windrider armor. "Let's head back toward Magix. Maybe we can get to Alfea from there."

A small part of Bloom was tempted to ask Sky to stay in the quiet clearing with her for a little while. It had not escaped her notice that they were completely alone together, and the feelings she had for the gorgeous blond prince were almost overwhelming, and quite confusing.

She wanted to ask him about the full story of his engagement to Princess Diaspro, wondering if his feelings for the powerful princess were as strong as—or stronger than—they were for her.

Even with all the questions she wanted to ask Sky, what Bloom really wanted was just to spend a little more time with him to get to know him better.

But Alfea College was in terrible danger, as were Bloom's closest friends. Sadly, she didn't have any time to spend on romance, not with the fate of the whole Magic Dimension hanging in the balance.

Sky and Bloom found a narrow trail into the thick forest and followed it, hoping it would lead to a sign of civilization . . . or maybe even Alfea itself.

They walked through the beautiful green vegetation of the magical forest, until Bloom started to lose track of how long they'd been hiking along the faint trail. Then, as they passed a pile of boulders covered with weeds, she thought she heard a voice calling her.

"Bloom," someone whispered, sounding like a breeze through the leaves.

Bloom paused, listening carefully, but she heard only the normal noises of the forest. "Sky," she asked, "did you hear that?"

Sky stopped and tilted his head to listen. "Hear what?"

"I thought I heard someone calling my name," Bloom replied, glancing around nervously.

"I didn't hear anything," Sky said. He started walking along the path again. "Come on, we've got to keep moving."

After only another few minutes, passing a cute, double-tailed orange squirrel scurrying along a tree branch, Bloom heard her named being called again.

"Bloom," the voice said softly, but more clearly this time, with more urgency. "Bloom!"

Grabbing Sky's arm and shoulder, Bloom halted him. "You must have heard that!" she insisted. "Someone is calling me!"

Sky glanced around, looking annoyed. "Bloom, I don't hear anything," he said. "Nobody is calling you."

"No, Sky," Bloom argued. "It's real. It's *Daphne*. She's calling me." Bloom had only met the elegant nymph fairy once, in a vision Miss Faragonda had shown her, but she was sure she recognized the voice of her underwater fairy sister.

"Bloom," Sky sighed, "that's crazy."

"No, it's not," Bloom said. "I have to go to Lightrock Lake. Daphne's my sister, and I can hear her calling to me."

The Trix witches were the ones who had told Bloom that Daphne was her sister, but they had also said that ancient diabolical witches had gotten rid of Daphne forever. Then Miss Faragonda had magically shown Bloom the magnificently beautiful depths of Lightrock Lake, where her sister lived. The Trix had lied. Daphne was alive, and she needed Bloom.

"Well, then," Sky decided, "I'm going with you."

Bloom pressed her hand against his muscular chest. "No, Sky," she said firmly, "I must go alone.

71

You go on to Alfea. I'll catch up." She turned and strode away, quickly vanishing into the dark forest.

Sky wasn't sure he should let her go. It wasn't safe for Bloom to be wandering around the woods alone, especially without her powers. But she had seemed so certain that he hadn't been able to argue.

There were probably perfect words to convince her to stay with him, or to let him go with her, but Sky hadn't been able to think of them in time.

"Oh, man," Sky swore, before continuing on the narrow trail out of the forest.

CHAPTER
11

Over at Alfea College, plans for the battle with the Trix were nearly ready. The wizards, witches, and fairies had hastily developed defensive spells and practiced attack magic. At the moment, the school grounds were quiet as everyone mentally prepared for the fight. It was the calm before the storm.

The Winx had gathered to rest and chat in their suite, but Stella felt too uneasy to relax. She stood leaning on the railing of the balcony outside the main room, wondering if her friend was in danger.

"I hope Bloom's okay," she whispered, wishing there were something she could do to help. She felt powerless, and she hated that feeling. She heaved a deep sigh before turning around to stride inside.

In the Winx's living room, Stella found Flora, Musa, and Tecna standing around a long table, staring thoughtfully at a plump orange pumpkin resting on a bed of green leaves.

"Oh, poor Mirta," said Stella.

The pumpkin wasn't a normal, everyday gourd. It had once been a young witch named Mirta, who had risked her life to defy the Trix and tell Bloom about their evil plans to trick her. She had defended Bloom against the evil witches in a battle, too, but the Trix had transformed her into the pretty pumpkin now sitting on the Winx's table.

The Winx desperately wanted to restore the brave witch to life, but so far nothing they had come up with had broken the spell. Because Flora was the Fairy of Nature, it had fallen to her to lead the attempt to turn Mirta back into a teenage girl.

"Flora," Musa said firmly, "you can't give up!"

"You are the only one who can help her," added Tecna matter-of-factly.

Stella nodded, smiling with encouragement at her nurturing friend. "You have to bring her back."

"You can do it, Flora," Musa insisted.

Flora squinted in determination. "I'll try," she said.

Stepping closer to the pumpkin, Flora held her palms over the pumpkin, stroking the long leaves cascading from its stem. Then she called up her powers, her hands glowing with bright yellow light. The other Winx jumped back, alarmed by the intensity of Flora's brilliant power and the way her eyes were blazing yellow.

Flora sent her spirit deep into the pumpkin, entering a mystical realm where Nature revealed Mirta's true form. Flora was surrounded by fiery washes of saffron radiance. Then she saw Mirta as a teenage girl, bobbing in the scintillating glow, looking frightened, lost, and alone.

"Okay, Mirta," Flora breathed, extending her hand toward the young witch. "Reach out. . . . Take my hand. . . ."

Mirta floated closer, stretching her arm toward Flora.

Flora stretched, too . . . and intertwined her fingers with Mirta's, clasping the girl's hand.

Stella, Musa, and Tecna gasped, blinded momentarily as the pumpkin seemed to explode with yellow brilliance. Radiant sparkles showered the table, and the pumpkin vanished in a blaze of shimmering light.

"Mirta?" Flora whispered, worried.

But then the teenage witch materialized, standing beside the table, surrounded by sparks of glittering yellow. She had cropped magenta hair and was wearing the T-shirt with a pumpkin printed on it that she'd had on when the Trix transformed her. Mirta glanced at her own hands and let out a happy laugh.

"Mirta!" Flora cheered. "Oh, Mirta, you're back!"

Mirta rushed over to Flora and gave her a big hug, then spun her around in a joyful dance. "Oh, thank you, Flora," she said, hugging the fairy again. "Thank you for not giving up on me. You saved me!"

Flora broke their embrace and held the teenage witch's hands. "You were a really great pumpkin, Mirta," she said, laughing, "but I think I like you better as a person!"

Up at the spooky top of Cloudtower, the Trix gathered in Miss Griffin's office, standing around the big beetle with the scrying eye in its back. They focused their energies to spy into Alfea, and the grotesque eyeball flickered with pictures . . . including an image of Miss Faragonda and Miss Griffin making plans together.

"So, Miss Griffin is at Alfea," Icy muttered as the beetle closed its back and marched away.

Stormy frowned deeply. "They're ganging up on us!" she whined.

"It doesn't matter," said Darcy. She clenched her gloved hand into a fist. "We have the power of the Dragon Flame."

Icy raised her sharp eyebrows, her eyes glinting

with malice. "And it's time to use it," she declared. "We'll destroy them!"

High above the spires of Cloudtower, the flying beasts howled as they circled the castle, and the storm whirling above them raged harder.

"Creatures of the Dark!" Icy commanded. *"Arise!"*

Heeding Icy's command, thousands of repulsive creatures marched out of Cloudtower and assembled in the fields in front of the school. Some of the monsters had mutated even more, and now there were even bigger beasts, some with vicious lobster claws, some built like headless tanks with spiked legs, and some that had rows and rows of awful gnashing teeth. These were surrounded by an untold number of small centipede-like critters, roiling balls of purple worms, and unspeakably hideous crawling things with pig snouts and tentacles.

As the monsters lined up in the fields, the flying fiends circled overhead, cawing furiously, opening and closing their claws in the air as though they couldn't wait to begin the battle.

Three of the largest beasts stood tall amid the festering mass of creatures and allowed themselves to be overrun with worms and centipedes, which climbed their legs and bodies. Their heads became vast pyramids of wriggling evil. The pyramids grew higher into the sky and then three fused together, creating stepped, spiked towers with a throne on top of each.

The Trix flew over their army, hovering near the three lofty purple towers, eyeing them with pride.

"Come, sisters!" Icy declared, and she, Darcy, and Stormy swooped in to take their seats on the high thrones.

As soon as they were seated, the entire misshapen army let out a roar and started to march down the main road. In the middle of the churning mass of monsters, the towers scuttled forward on hundreds of scampering legs, carrying their witches in prime positions of ultimate power.

Icy grinned coldly. Her army of darkness was the greatest force ever assembled in the magical realm. She knew they were unstoppable.

"To Alfea!" Icy screeched, and the heinous army stomped onward, heading for the only place that stood between the Trix and total victory over the world.

CHAPTER
12

Meanwhile, Prince Sky had managed to find a way through the forest to Magix City, the most populated city in all of Magix. Tired from his long hike, he walked in through the beautiful city's tall gates, which surprisingly were unguarded and swinging open with eerie squeaks. In fact, as Sky wandered the wide avenues, he didn't see a single person, and the only movement was wind blowing trash and debris down the streets.

Magix City was deserted.

"Hello?" Sky hollered. "Is anybody here?"

But he received no reply.

The last time Sky had been in Magix City, it had been a bustling magical metropolis, filled with well-dressed people running around on errands, children playing, busy shops selling expensive wares, tourists from all over the magical realm milling about, and street vendors hawking charms and potions and mouthwatering sweet and savory treats.

Something terrible must have happened for the people of Magix to abandon their city.

"Can anyone hear me?" shouted Sky. He stopped in a town square near a pile of broken furniture, scanning the area for any signs of life.

A disgusting pig-snouted beast with dozens of tentacles flailing out of its mouth stepped from the shadows behind Sky and grunted at him. The creature was two or three times Sky's height and was encased in shiny purple armor covered with nasty spikes.

Luckily, Sky heard the monster before it got too close. "Huh?" he muttered, then whirled around, his blue energy sword blazing and ready to strike.

Sky ducked when the creature swung a sharp claw at him, but missed with his own sword lunge. Then the beast slammed his pincers downward, knocking the sword out of Sky's grasp.

The energy sword's blade fizzled out as its pommel bounced down the empty street. Sky dove after it, rolling and grabbing the sword as he tumbled back to his feet. He quickly ignited the blade again, dropping down in ready position to counter the beast's next attack.

"Come on!" Sky taunted the vile monster. "I'm not afraid of you!"

Hundreds of centipede critters scrambled toward the beast, disappearing into its feet as the larger creature absorbed them. The monster swelled in size, looming larger and larger above Sky's head, until he was standing entirely in its misshapen shadow.

Then the gargantuan monster roared wrathfully, wriggling its toxic mouth tentacles and raising its vast, gleaming claws to destroy the handsome prince.

On a broad rooftop of Alfea's tallest building, a squad of Specialists kept watch for any sign of the Trix's attack. The young wizards marched from ledge to ledge, peering over the edge into the surrounding forests at every stop. Some watched the storm clouds overhead for an indication that an attack would soon begin. Other Specialists guarded the rooftop perimeter, keeping their red swords and shields at the ready, while fairies swooped among the troops, carrying information and supplies.

Also on the rooftop were Miss Faragonda and Miss Griffin, keeping careful watch over the front gate from their high perch.

"They're coming," Miss Griffin said. "I can feel it."

Miss Faragonda nodded. "Yes. I know."

Moments later, the storm clouds darkened and lightning split the sky. The Specialists rushed to line up in formation in the courtyard, gripping their energy sword pommels tightly.

Mr. Saladin and Mr. Codatorta stood with their student wizards on the front lines, ready to join in the fight with their potent magic and experienced swordsmanship.

Stella, Musa, Tecna, and Bloom hovered near Miss Faragonda, prepared to use their fairy powers any way they could to defend their school and the people in it.

Lightning zigzagged across the dark sky again, and the first loathsome creatures in the Trix's army scuttled into view down the long main road to the front gates.

"All right, this is it," declared Headmistress Faragonda, her voice magically echoing through Alfea. "Hold your positions, everyone!" She narrowed her eyes behind her glasses, glaring at the approaching army. "The stakes have never been higher."

On their three purple towers at the center of their invading army, the Trix reclined casually, enjoying the trip with insolent pride. The creatures along the road were hundreds deep on each side, and thousands more stretched out behind them. Overhead, the winged beasts fluttered and flapped and crowed shrilly in their lust for battle.

Just to make her point absolutely clear, Icy conjured up a glowing green sphere of command

and used it to direct the Trix's army toward the fairy college. "Alfea!" she ordered, grinning evilly.

The appalling beasts reached the walls of the school, gathering outside the gates. The three witches' towers blotted out swaths of the sky, looming taller than Alfea's highest building.

For a long moment, the Trix held their vicious horde still and silent outside the gates, the better to build up terror in the desperately outnumbered defenders of Alfea.

Calmly, as though she were muttering a mild greeting, Icy murmured, "Attack."

At her offhand command, the beasts and crawlies and creatures rushed the gates, and the flying monsters dove down, gnashing at the students with jaws full of razor-sharp teeth.

Icy sat up sharply as she saw Miss Faragonda and Miss Griffin duck attacks by winged beasts. Then the two headmistresses on their high rooftop launched a powerful green-glowing spell over the school grounds. Their defensive charm soared above

Alfea and exploded like fireworks, creating a thick, shimmering green protective dome of energy that descended around the edges of the college, keeping out the rampaging monsters.

Icy glared at the dome. Alfea was safe . . . as long as the magical shield held against the onslaught of the horde of malevolent creatures. Then Icy's mood changed as she realized that the magical shield couldn't hold for very long—not with the power of the Dragon Flame on the side of the Trix.

Icy smiled.

While the battle at Alfea raged, Bloom walked into an enchanted clearing that seemed straight out of a folktale. Glimmers of fairy dust sparkled through the gorgeous trees and delicate flowers around Lightrock Lake, which itself glittered blue in the dappled sunlight. Bullfrogs hopped on lily pads adorned with flowers, and a gentle, sweet-smelling breeze wafted around the lovely lake.

When the breeze ruffled Bloom's hair, her magical armor evaporated, leaving her in her cute, comfortable daily clothes. She waded into the cool water, her toes squishing deliciously in the sandy mud of the lakebed. "Daphne?" she asked, striding deeper toward the center of the lake. "I heard you calling me. I'm here."

"Bloom," whispered Daphne's serene voice. "Come to me, Bloom."

Feeling like she had entered a fabulous fantasy, Bloom stopped at the edge of a much deeper pool and stared into the clear water, looking down at the exotic underwater plants and ornate rock formations. Sandy paths led through arches into the unseen depths.

"Come to me," Daphne repeated. "Follow my voice."

Bloom stepped off the rocky ledge and let herself sink slowly into the water. She glided to the bottom of the lake, where amazing structures of rock rose all around, each carved into delicate patterns by the flowing liquid.

Then a slender, graceful fairy materialized in front of Bloom in a shimmer of light. She wore a harlequin's mask, and the folds of her elegant, glowing gown wavered in the water.

"Daphne," said Bloom, her red hair floating around her in tendrils, "am I dreaming?"

Daphne smiled. "No, Bloom," she said, "you're not dreaming." Rays of light streamed from her. "Come with me, little sister. You haven't lost your powers. Look over there." Daphne tilted her head toward a dark cave to her left, shiny with big bubbles that returned the fairy's light. "Look and see who you really are."

Nodding, Bloom turned and gazed at the bubbles.

"It's my home," she gasped as she saw a vision of herself riding a bicycle along the pretty streets of the town where she was raised. "Gardenia!"

Then the image shifted to her family house, where her mother and father snuggled together on a love seat. "And my parents," Bloom said. "I mean . . . my adoptive parents." She saw flashes of her father rescuing her from the fire as a baby, and herself blowing out the candles on her first birthday cake with her parents there to cheer her on, and then her mom and dad staring at her with love as she left them to go to Alfea College for the first time.

"Yes," Daphne replied, "your parents, who raised you, and who love you with all their hearts, as you love them. Now look closer, Bloom."

Daphne held out a small coral treasure chest shining with gorgeous jewels. "This is your birthright," she said, and the chest swung open, revealing an elegant pale green tiara that glowed softly. It was decorated with a large oval blue gem set in a magnificently flared front peak. "The crown of Domino." Daphne stared deeply into Bloom's wide green eyes. "You are a princess, Bloom."

Bloom couldn't believe it. Her? A princess? There was no way. "No," she said, bowing her head. "I am a failure. I let the Trix take my Dragon Flame."

Daphne shook her head gently. "Nobody can steal your past, your dreams, or your powers," she told the young fairy. "You just have to look deep inside yourself . . . and you will find them."

With those words, brilliant yellow light surrounded Daphne, blinding Bloom momentarily. By the time her vision had cleared, Daphne had vanished.

"Daphne?" Bloom called. "Daphne!"

She wandered around the lakebed paths for a few minutes but saw no sign of her mysterious fairy sister.

Bloom was on her own.

But she knew what she had to do next.

Chapter
13

For a short while, Lightrock Lake's surface stayed placid and sparkling in the sunlight. Then a joyful shout shattered the tranquility.

"Magix Winx!" Bloom exclaimed, her voice echoing through the clearing. "Charmix!"

She burst out of the lake, soaring on her gossamer wings. She was dressed in the green outfit she wore whenever she transformed into a powerful fairy.

Bloom blazed up into the sky, twirling with glee. Her magical abilities were back . . . or perhaps they had never been truly lost. All Bloom knew for certain was that she felt like her old self again.

No, she thought. I feel better than ever!

"Bloom!" she announced to herself. "Fairy of the Dragon Flame!"

Her power swirled around her in streaks of blazing red energy shaped like a fire-breathing dragon. It filled her with fierce determination and a sense that she could accomplish anything . . . if she only remembered who she truly was.

Now it was time to return to Alfea and show those awful Trix how love, family, and friendship could triumph over selfish evil.

Bloom streaked through the air like a mighty comet.

On her way to the fairy college, she passed over Magix City . . . and spotted someone familiar down on the deserted streets.

It was Sky!

And he was in big trouble.

Bloom swooped lower, heading toward Sky as he battled two giant beasts in an otherwise empty intersection. They threatened Sky from either side, and he defended himself with his energy sword.

Just when it seemed Sky had bashed the monsters back enough for him to escape, a gross purple creature materialized in the air to his right. It was another huge beast with mouth tentacles, and it dropped down, trapping Sky between the three monsters.

Bloom flew faster as the creatures advanced on Sky, who kept swinging his sword, even though it seemed not to dent their armor at all.

"I refuse to surrender!" Sky hollered. "I'll never give up!"

Bloom admired his bravery, but she could plainly see that he was in terrible danger of being overpowered at any moment. Gathering her magic around her in the shape of a glowing red dragon, she launched sizzling missiles of energy at the monster. One by one, she reduced them to ashes with her mighty magic.

"Huh?" Sky said, glancing around to see who had come to his rescue. "What in the world?" Then he looked up and saw Bloom, and his jaw dropped in amazement at the brilliant power radiating from her. "Bloom!"

Bloom fluttered down and hovered by his side. "Sky, are you all right?"

Sky smiled and held her hand. "Yes, now," he said softly. "Bloom . . . you saved my life."

With a pretty blush reddening her cheeks, Bloom squeezed his hand and then let go.

"Well," Sky said, suddenly sounding all business. "I guess we better get to Alfea. I bet they need your help."

"And yours," Bloom added.

At the fairy school, the dome of magical energy protecting Alfea was under constant attack by the winged creatures above and the hideous beasts below. Inside, the fairies, Specialists, and witches watched nervously, hoping the barrier would hold.

From atop her tall purple tower, Stormy laughed hard, enjoying the fact that the shield was starting to fizzle from the unrelenting waves of creatures of darkness bashing into it.

"Do they really think their silly barrier can stop us?" Stormy wondered, standing on her tower. She conjured up the intense power she'd copied from Bloom, and the outline of a purple dragon glowed electrically around her momentarily. Then she focused her magical energy and shot an enormous, blistering bolt of lightning at the dome.

Irreparably damaged from all the monsters' attacks, the dome couldn't withstand Stormy's mighty lightning. Everyone inside screamed as the shield shimmered faintly and then blinked out under the force of the blast.

The flying creatures were the first to break through, dive-bombing the defenders, avoiding the Specialists' swords, and snapping at the fairies with their horrible gnashing teeth.

"Oh, no!" Musa screamed. But then her bravery asserted itself, and she tightened her hands into fists, shaking them in determination at the attackers. She rushed over to Stella, Flora, and Tecna, and they quickly huddled together, shouting in unison the spell that activated their amazing powers, "Magic Winx! Charmix!"

The four fairies raised their arms above their heads as scintillating light in every color of the rainbow swirled around them. Magical energy poured into the girls, making them shine like stars gone supernova.

One by one, they summoned their specific abilities:

"Musa! Fairy of Music!"

"Stella! Fairy of the Shining Sun!"

"Flora! Fairy of Nature!"

"Tecna! Fairy of Technology!"

As each Winx declared her name and power, she became clothed in her battle outfit and radiated with awesomely vibrant illumination.

"You've got it coming, you evil witches!" Flora yelled, and she created a small, twinkling spark in her hand that looked like a spinning flower. Flora blew on the spark, and it sped right toward Stormy on her tall tower.

Stormy grunted loudly as she blocked Flora's spark with her glowing hand, anticipating a powerful attack. But the flowery spark just lingered for a second, glittering on Stormy's fingertips, doing no damage. "What's this?" she said dismissively, and she flicked away the spark, sneering.

For a second, Flora felt insulted by her inability to hurt Stormy, but there was too much happening for her to dwell on it.

With the dome down, the atrocious purple creatures charged the gates, smashing through them, stampeding into the school grounds. Alfea was being overrun!

Student witches attacked the beasts with spells while teen fairies gathered in groups to pool their magic and blast rows of creepy centipedes. Squads of Specialists fired starlight blasters from the balcony of tall buildings while other wizards fired energy crossbows at the flying creatures.

But for every monster the students or their instructors destroyed, it seemed like there were a dozen to take its place.

The Winx stood on the front lines, frying critters with their magical attacks. Tecna zapped a beast with her technology beams, but Stella took a few steps backward, worried about their defenses.

"We can't hold them!" Stella groaned. "They're breaking though!"

Atop her purple tower, Icy stood and surveyed the destruction in front of her, cackling happily. Her army was breaching Alfea's pathetic barricades, and soon she would rule this school, too—

Icy gasped in shock as fiery explosions detonated in the sky among her flying critters, destroying dozens at once. Then a huge wall of orange flame rose, scorching most of the remainder of her aerial assault force.

Bloom had arrived in the nick of time. She hovered over the city, surrounded by flickering flames as her dragon power entwined around her.

"It's Bloom!" Stella shouted happily. *"Yahoo!"*

With a big smile, Bloom waved at the cheering students in Alfea, saving a special wink for the Winx.

"Well, hi, everybody!" she called down. "You mind if I join in?"

CHAPTER
14

In the courtyard, Sky had sneaked past the invaders and found his squad of Specialists.

"Hey, Sky!" Brandon exclaimed. "It sure is good to see you!" He, Riven, and Timmy all clapped Sky on the back, thrilled that their team of friends was together again.

Icy held her arms straight down and clenched her fists in pure frustration, glaring with fury at Bloom floating above Alfea. "It's not possible!" Icy screeched.

"I can't believe this!" Stormy wailed.

Darcy simply looked very, very nervous.

Bloom soared closer to the Trix on their towers. Glowing beams blazed out from her in every direction.

"Thought you'd gotten rid of me, right?" she asked the evil witches. "Well, you thought wrong!"

She called up her Dragon Flame again, and the mythical reptile wrapped itself around her. Then Bloom conjured up an enormous fireball and hurled it right at Icy.

Icy screamed and had to leap out of the way. The fireball exploded on her throne, annihilating the top of her tower.

Stormy and Darcy quickly joined Icy floating in the air above the battle.

"Well, look who's back," Icy sneered, pretending to be unimpressed. "Let's give her a *cold* welcome."

Down on the school grounds, Stella groaned, "Enough already with the evil!"

"Come on, Winx!" Tecna shouted, and she, Stella, Flora, and Musa took to the sky to help Bloom any way they could . . . and to make life a little more difficult for the Trix.

When Icy saw the other Winx joining Bloom in the air, she rolled her eyes. "Oh, look," she taunted, "more fairies. But . . . so what?" Icy opened her fist and a whirling wheel of snow spun out. It formed a funnel and swirled right at the Winx.

Flora let out a little shriek, but Bloom countered the frozen attack with a blast of fiery plasma, which melted the snow and knocked the Trix off balance.

Now that Icy was separated from her sisters, Bloom rocketed right at her and chased her down toward the lake on Alfea's outskirts. Icy skidded backward across the lake's surface, dodging Bloom's small fireballs.

Meanwhile, the battle at the fairy school was worse than ever. The hideous creatures had ripped apart Alfea's walls and were now free to run wild through the school grounds. Specialists shot at the beasts with their starlight blasters while other wizards battled the monsters on the ground with their swords. They all fought with intense courage, even if they had no hope of winning a hand-to-hand war.

In the courtyard, Riven smacked a tentacle-mouthed monster with his energy bolt, then sizzled another with his glowing dagger. He took a few steps backward to get a better vantage point and bumped right into Sky.

"Hey," Sky greeted his friend.

They quickly fell into a pattern of fighting back-to-back so no monster could get the jump on them.

"Where in the world did you and Bloom go?" Riven asked as he fought a horde of centipedes.

Sky struck out with his energy sword, keeping the nasty creatures at bay. "We parked the windrider in the Dark Forest," he replied, "and we went for a walk."

"So," Riven panted, "how'd it go?"

"Well," Sky answered, slicing a flying monster that tried to buzz him, "we wanted to be alone . . . and believe me, we were. Magix City is a total ghost town, Riven!"

Riven glanced up at the sky, where Stormy and Darcy were overseeing the mayhem at the school. "The Trix have outdone themselves this time," he growled.

"Yeah," Sky replied. "I think Bloom has just about had it with them."

Then they both had to concentrate on fighting off an armored beast roaring at them.

Above the college, Flora, Musa, Tecna, and Stella bravely challenged Stormy and Darcy. Stella growled at the two Trix.

In response, Darcy multiplied herself four times. The four new Darcies hovered in a line. Stormy and Darcy pooled their powers and created a whirlwind vortex shimmering with flashes of lightning along its length. The vortex spun right toward the Winx, so Tecna conjured up a green vector cage in a sphere around herself and her friends. With Tecna focusing hard, the vector cage repelled the vortex, but the sphere dissolved in the attack.

Stella swung her long staff at the Trix, hurling a ball of sunshine at them that singed their hair and wiped out Darcy's duplicate selves.

Then Flora hollered, "Flower Twister!" She blasted the Trix with a spiral of glowing petals, which didn't seem to affect the witches.

"Let's add a touch of music to this!" cried Musa. She held up her fingers, and two magical stereo speakers appeared on either side of the Trix, blasting them with sonic squawks.

Covering her ears, Stormy screamed, "All right, that's enough!" She destroyed the speakers with purple lightning bolts.

Darcy knocked the Winx back with concentric circles of power, and for a while, the Trix and the Winx traded mild explosive attacks, with nobody seeming to get the upper hand.

Finally, they all broke apart, panting. The Trix glared at the Winx while they hovered in the sky.

Then Stormy smiled at Darcy. "Sister," she said, "I'm going to blow those fairies away!"

Darcy hurried off to the side while Stormy stretched out her arms and started to spin like a whirligig. A gray tornado twisted around her, flashing with jags of purple lightning. This cyclone was superior to any Stormy had created before—it stretched all the way to the ground, and was wide and violently fast.

When the tornado's tip touched the courtyard, it ripped up flagstones and hurled Specialists off their feet. Miss Faragonda gasped as it blurred past the tower top where she and Miss Griffin were fighting off flying beasts.

Up at the wider part of the whirling funnel, the Winx tried to fly away from the twister, but its pull was too strong. The fairies got sucked in and were tossed every which way. Flora was affected the worst—she flipped into the center of the vortex and passed out.

Musa and Stella kicked and swam through the wild winds, desperate to reach their friend. "Flora!" screamed Stella as she spun around the unconscious fairy. She gritted her teeth and stretched out her hand, reaching for Flora to try to save her from the tornado's whirling maw.

Stella grabbed Flora's hand, and Flora woke up. Together they wrenched themselves out of the funnel and joined Tecna and Musa just outside the tornado. All four of them grabbed Stella's long staff of the Sun and held on, and as a group they cast a quick spell, all of them suddenly glowing golden.

The power of the four fairies working as friends wrested control of the tornado away from Stormy, and the lightning flickering along the tunnel's spinning winds turned from purple to yellow.

The Winx now commanded the tornado!

The fairies sent the vortex back after its creator, and Stormy squealed. "Oh, no!" she cried as she tried to escape the violent twister. She and Darcy smashed into the funnel, and the tornado winked out of existence as both teen witches plummeted toward the ground far below.

Taking advantage of the Trix's momentary powerlessness, Miss Faragonda and Miss Griffin each blasted a brilliant energy beam from their hands, the fairy headmistress's blue magic mixing with the witch headmistress's fiery yellow beam of power. Together the two professors created a huge iron ball covered with spikes around the Trix, trapping them inside.

The spiked iron ball fell straight down, crashing with a solid thud into the courtyard, where it buried itself halfway into the dirt.

The Winx landed around the iron ball, exhausted and panting. Miss Faragonda and Miss Griffin hurried over. The headmistresses checked inside. Darcy and Stormy were alive, and the magic prison would hold them tight for as long as necessary.

Two of the Trix had been defeated.

CHAPTER
15

Above the lake on the outskirts of Alfea, Bloom faced off against the remaining wicked Trix, Icy. The formidable witch and the mighty fairy circled each other in the sky, with zigs and zags of lightning illuminating the storm raging around them.

Bloom grunted as she summoned her dragonfire and sent it shooting out toward Icy. But the witch was ready for her, and froze the dragonfire, exploding it in thick shards of ice. Glaring at Bloom furiously, Icy commanded her snowy powers and chased the fairy across the lake with a funnel of shimmering frost.

To avoid being frozen in the frigid funnel, Bloom had to flip and tumble and dodge in the air. She headed for a stand of tall trees and let the frosty power hit them instead. Then Bloom teleported herself in a bright flash back over to Icy.

"That the best you got, witchy-poo?" taunted Bloom, her hands on her hips defiantly as she hovered in front of the last Trix.

In reply, Icy screamed out a ferocious spell, launching dozens of frozen missiles at the fairy.

Bloom glowed with fiery intensity, easily melting the cold projectiles.

But Icy wasn't done. She narrowed her eyes and instantly encased Bloom in a block of ice. Then the witch added iced spikes to the block, which caused it to drop from the sky like a meteor. The block tumbled down and smashed into the main road, exploding into millions of ice chips.

Icy laughed, certain she had just totally crushed Bloom.

Her laugh cut off sharply when Bloom suddenly materialized right behind her shoulder. She had teleported safely out of the ice block before it hit the ground. Bloom giggled and sassily flashed Icy a peace sign with her fingers. Then Bloom blasted Icy out of the air with a pulse of flaming dragonfire.

Icy tumbled down into the lake, but she wasn't nearly defeated. Immediately, a giant ice-water hand stretched out of the lake and grabbed Bloom. It pulled her down under the water while Icy zoomed back into the air.

Shaking off droplets, Icy spun a funnel of snow at the lake, freezing the entire surface, trapping Bloom beneath a thick layer of ice. Icy laughed gleefully, positive that this time she'd gotten rid of Bloom once and for all.

In the middle of the frozen lake, the ice cracked. Bloom broke through, blazing from head to toe with fiery might, and rose to challenge Icy again.

Icy shook with fury and frustration. She flung her arms outward and screeched, "I'm taking you down . . . now!" Icy conjured up her biggest snow funnel yet, a vast, swirling column filled with a whirling blizzard. It stretched from the surface of the lake all the way up to the clouds, and at Icy's command, it started to solidify in great jagged spikes of ice.

Bloom squealed as she was caught in the spikes, which rapidly multiplied around her, forming an enormous tower of gnarled ice that rose out of the lake many times higher than the tallest building at Alfea.

Icy cackled happily, pointing her finger at the frozen tower. "Shake that one off, fairy!" she sneered.

For a long moment, it seemed as though Icy had won. Who in the Magic Dimension could free herself from such an unbelievably massive amount of ice? It would take unimaginable abilities to break out of a frozen prison the size of a mountain.

But Bloom had the power of the Dragon Flame within her.

A giant burning dragon burst out of the lake and wrapped itself three times around the ice tower. The dragon roared at Icy and then squeezed the tower like a boa constrictor, crushing it to powder.

Now free, Bloom glowed all over, as if she contained the sun. Moaning with effort, she pulled in her arms and legs, contracting herself as she concentrated all her power at once. Then she expanded abruptly, radiating so intensely that she lit up all of the Dark Forest surrounding Alfea. Rays of her fiery power shone for a mile around, blasting the disgusting creatures of darkness everywhere, obliterating them with awesome energy.

Icy vanished in the explosion of fire.

Still radiating, Bloom created a dome around Alfea that withered and destroyed all the beasts within, snuffing them out in puffs of smoke. The flying creatures fried in the air, annihilated by Bloom's might.

Then the blazing dome over Alfea disappeared, and Bloom's light suddenly winked out.

Down in the school courtyard, all the defenders gaped in amazement at the display of power they had just witnessed. The monsters were gone. Alfea was safe.

But where was the amazing fairy who had saved them all?

"Bloom," Miss Faragonda whispered worriedly.

Stormy, standing next to Darcy, also whispered Bloom's name, but she did it with a growl, as though swearing revenge. Miss Faragonda had put magical handcuffs on Stormy and Darcy and taken them out of their metal prison.

Prince Sky stood between Brandon and Riven, searching the air for any sign of Bloom. For a long while, the school remained hushed as everyone waited to see if Bloom had sacrificed herself to save Alfea . . . or if she had survived.

Then, without fanfare, Bloom floated down toward the courtyard. She was carrying Icy, who was unconscious in her arms.

"Yeah!" Specialists, witches, and fairies throughout Alfea hollered. "All right!"

Bloom flew over to the headmistresses and the

headmaster of the magical schools and laid Icy down in front of them. "Here you go, Miss Faragonda," said Bloom sweetly.

After a second, Icy groaned and sat up, her cheeks wet with green tears from her runny mascara. She flinched, startled at where she found herself.

"Young lady," Miss Faragonda scolded, "you and your sisters have behaved very badly."

Miss Griffin raised an eyebrow. "That's putting it mildly, Faragonda."

"And so—" Miss Faragonda began.

"You will be confined to Lightrock Monastery," Miss Griffin broke in, "until we see fit to release you."

The Winx rushed over to Bloom and crowded around her, jostling her with joyful hugs.

"Hey!" Stella cheered, giving Bloom a kiss on the cheek. "You did great!"

"Oh, Bloom!" Flora gushed happily.

Tecna nodded in admiration. "You melted Icy."

Bloom gasped. Over Stella's shoulder, she saw Sky approaching with a big smile on his face. "Sky," she breathed.

"Bloom!" exclaimed Sky, his blue eyes twinkling with delight at seeing her alive.

"Excuse me," Stella said cheerfully, stepping to the side so Bloom could reunite with the handsome blond Specialist.

Sky's expression suddenly became intensely serious. He closed his eyes and leaned forward to kiss Bloom ever so sweetly on the lips. Then he laughed, thrilled to be with her again, and they wrapped each other in a warm embrace.

On the other side of the courtyard, Miss Faragonda and Miss Griffin walked together through the wrecked school grounds, surveying the damage the Trix had done with their awful army.

"Those young witches nearly destroyed Magix," said Miss Griffin. She sounded almost apologetic.

Miss Faragonda stopped walking and turned to face the other headmistress. "The Trix are dangerous," she replied.

Nodding, Miss Griffin said, "Let's see what a nice long stay in a bright and cheerful monastery does for them."

Nearby, burly Specialist guards flanked Darcy, Stormy, and Icy as they marched them into a glowing blue dimensional portal to escort them to the monastery. Before she entered the portal, Icy paused and glared over her shoulder with pure hatred at Bloom and the Winx.

Stella waved at Icy, returning her glare with a big smile. "Buh-bye!" she called cheerfully.

Bloom met Icy's gaze with firm determination of her own. If Icy ever returned to wreak more havoc, Bloom would be waiting for her—and she'd stop the evil witch again if necessary!

That night, as a serene darkness fell over Alfea, the fairies, Specialists, and witches threw a giant party in the courtyard. Music blasted all over the school, and flashing fairy lights and glowing multicolored orbs illuminated happily dancing students. Everyone enjoyed delicious food and drink as they celebrated their victory over the Trix.

In the center of the courtyard, Bloom raised her glass of sparkling nectar for a toast. She was surrounded by her best friends, the Winx, and the Specialists in Sky's squad. "Here's to us!" said Bloom, and her friends cheered merrily.

"Yay!" sang Musa.

With joyful students dancing behind her, Flora smiled. "Who would have ever thought that we would all be here safe and sound?" she asked.

"And celebrating!" added Tecna as she was passed a plate heaped with delicious fruit.

Knut grabbed a chunk of watermelon and gobbled it, and the Winx and the Specialists laughed heartily.

Later, after the party had calmed, Bloom found a quiet spot and sat on the edge of a fountain where she could look over the gorgeous lake sparkling in the silvery moonlight. Lost in contemplation, she didn't hear Sky approaching until he was near her.

"Bloom," Sky asked softly, "are you okay?"

Bloom nodded. "Yes," she replied. "I'm just thinking."

"About what?" asked Sky, sitting beside her on the stone rim of the fountain.

"Everything," Bloom answered. "How crazy the Trix are, how great my friends are, how much I've learned . . . how much I've changed." She smiled a little sadly. "I wonder what's going to happen next?"

Sky slid his hand over to Bloom's. "I don't know," he said, intertwining his fingers with hers. "But I guess we'll find out . . . together."

As Bloom sat beside Sky, holding his warm, comforting hand, she saw a shooting star streak across the moon. She sighed and leaned against Sky's shoulder, and this time her smile held nothing but happiness.